Curious George Likes Dinosaurs

Written by Francie Alexander

Houghton Mifflin Harcourt
Boston   New York

George is a curious monkey.
George likes dinosaurs.
Look at the dinosaurs in
George's book.

Some dinosaurs were big.
Some dinosaurs were small.

Look.
Curious George and his
friends will see dinosaurs
at the museum.

George looks and points
to the dinosaur bones.

All dinosaurs are born from eggs.

George wishes he could touch the dinosaur.
No, George. Just look.

George is at home now.
He can see more dinosaurs
on the computer.
He points to the screen.

Curious George likes dinosaurs.
He likes to look at them in
books.
He likes to look at them at the
museum.
He likes to look at them on the
computer.

Look—here is a dinosaur
George can touch.
Sweet dreams, Curious George.